CLASSIC STAR WARS®

A New Hope™

Read all the books in the Classic Star Wars® trilogy!

A NEW HOPE™
THE EMPIRE STRIKES BACK™
RETURN OF THE JEDI™

CLASSIC

STAR WARS®

A New Hope™

Adapted by Larry Weinberg
from the screenplay by George Lucas

Bullseye Books
Random House New York

A BULLSEYE BOOK PUBLISHED BY RANDOM HOUSE, INC.

 Published in the United States by Random House, Inc., New York, and simultaneously in Canada by Random House of Canada Limited, Toronto. Originally published by Random House, Inc., in 1985.

Library of Congress Catalog Number: 94-69163
ISBN: 0-679-87203-5
RL: 2.7

First Random House Bullseye Books edition: 1995

Manufactured in the United States of America 10 9 8 7 6 5 4 3

PROLOGUE

Long ago and far, far away there was an evil empire. It ruled over a whole galaxy. A few Rebel planets tried to break free of it. But the power of the Emperor was vast. And in command of his army was the mightiest warrior of them all.

CHAPTER ONE

Across the blackness of space a great warship chased its enemy. Darth Vader was in command. He did not speak as he watched. He did not have to. His troopers knew they must not fail to capture the Rebel ship.

Now the gap was closing. Vader lifted his hand. It was the signal to fire. Killer beams shot out at the smaller craft. The fleeing vessel zigged and zagged. But it could not escape. One after another the laser bolts hit their target. The Rebel ship bounced and shook. Its guns could no longer fight back. It was helpless.

Vader dropped his hand. The firing stopped. His deep voice rumbled like thunder. "Soon the stolen plans for the Death Star will be back in my hands. Then the Empire will destroy the Rebellion. Once and for all."

Inside the Rebel craft the captain led his men into the main passageway. "On the double! They'll be blasting their way in here any second. Where is Princess Leia?"

"Right here!" Leia came out of her cabin with a laser pistol in her hands.

"Quick!" said the captain. "Climb into the escape pod. It will take you down to Tatooine. My men will cover you until you get away."

"No! I'll stay here and fight!"

"You can't! You'll be killed. And the Rebel Alliance is counting on you. You've got to take them the secret plans!"

"I have to send the plans off without me," Leia replied. "The Imperials know I have them. If I stay here, I can stall them until the pod gets away. But I'll need a robot to take the plans to the Alliance. One of your best droids!"

"Use the R2-D2 unit," said the captain. "I saw it around here."

Suddenly an explosion rocked the ship. Clouds of smoke poured down the passageway. Through it came the Dark Lord's troops, firing their blasters. The captain raced back to his men. Princess Leia hurried off to find the droid.

Moments later someone else went looking for the R2-D2. It was See-Threepio, a robot shaped like a man. "Artoo!" he cried. "Oh, this is terrible! Artoo-Detoo, where are you? Do answer me!"

"Boing, boing, ping!"

It was Artoo squeaking. Threepio turned and saw the round little robot. He was standing in a darkened room. Was that a young woman bending over him? Threepio was too upset to tell. For now Vader's troops were rushing in with drawn blasters.

"Look!" cried a sergeant. "There's the Rebel woman that Lord Vader wants us to capture. Don't kill her. Set for stun."

Before the troopers could fire, Leia blasted them. Two troopers fell. She started to run. The sergeant took aim. His blast caught her! She went down in a heap.

The soldiers lifted her up. They didn't even look at the droids. What for? They were only robots. Silently Artoo rolled away on his little wheels.

Threepio hurried after him. "Where are you going now?" he cried.

"Bleep. Grr-whirr. Ping...ping...ding," the little droid squeaked.

"Mission? What mission? Wait! Why are you going into that docking bay? Droids aren't allowed—"

The computer in Threepio's head was all in a whirl. He couldn't believe it. Artoo was rolling himself into one of the tiny escape capsules!

"Hey!" he called. "Droids are not allowed in those. You'll be punished! Turned into scrap metal!"

"Brreep, poing, wurbul-urm."

"Don't you dare call me a ninny! And no! I am not going in there with you!"

Another explosion came from the other end of the ship. Then, from everywhere at once, there were cracking, snapping noises. It sounded as if the ship were coming apart! Threepio decided not to fuss about rules. He jumped into the pod.

One of Artoo's metal arms reached out to start the controls. With a roar the pod blasted free of the doomed Rebel ship.

Aboard Vader's ship, gunners took aim. But the officer in charge saw no reason to shoot down the little pod. "My scanner shows there are no life forms aboard. A short circuit must have sent it off by mistake."

The Dark Lord soon learned that he had a prisoner but no stolen plans. Then he heard about the escape pod. "Princess Leia must have hidden the plans inside it," he told one of his men. "Send a landing party to the planet. Bring me back those plans!"

"We shall, my lord."

"As for the princess—she shall serve us

yet. I will use her to find and destroy the Rebels' hidden base."

"She will die before she tells you anything."

"We shall see," growled Vader.

CHAPTER TWO

The escape pod hit the ground with a thud.

"Must you drive so roughly?" cried Threepio. "You've rattled my insides. I am a very carefully made machine!"

He got out behind Artoo and gazed around. "Oh, no! Just look where you've landed us. In the middle of a desert! Artoo, how could you!"

The little droid spun his top around until one of his bulbs lit up. Then off he went.

Threepio followed, grumbling.

"Pling, plang, plong!" beeped Artoo.

"All right, all right. I won't say another word. Go ahead, get us lost!"

Onward they went in silence. The day grew hotter and hotter. Threepio felt as if he were going to melt. "I simply have to rest before I fall apart," he gasped. "Let's stop now."

"Blurp, blurb, wur-beep," said Artoo.

"Don't tell me any more about missions! I asked you to stop!"

Artoo did stop. He spun his top until the bulb lit again. The off he went, whistling like a metal bird.

The heat was giving Threepio a terrible temper. "You know what?" he snapped. "I've had just about enough of you! You go your way, and I'll go mine!" And he set off alone across the sand dunes.

Artoo headed for some high rocks. But once he got there he moved slowly and carefully. There was something scary about this place.

"Gleep," he said softly to himself. "Gleep, gleep..."

He never saw the ray gun until it blasted in his face. Then everything seemed to explode. He could hear himself sizzle and crackle. Then he tipped forward and fell with a clang. Tiny jabbering creatures called Jawas lifted Artoo into a huge machine—a sandcrawler. They threw him down among a lot of other robots and went out.

"Gleep," beeped Artoo, looking around. He saw that most of the droids were in pieces.

"Artoo? Is that you?"

Out of a pile of robot parts rose Threepio. "Oh, I'm so glad to see you again!" And he threw his arms around his little friend.

The great machine started to move. “Does anyone know where they are taking us?” Threepio asked the other robots. “I’ve heard these Jawas sell droids to the farmers. Is that true?”

No one answered Threepio. But moments later the sandcrawler stopped. And Jawas began dragging their prisoners outside. Then they lined them up.

Artoo rolled out. He saw Threepio standing in a line of droids.

Two men were walking down the line, looking at the droids. “Snap out of it, Luke,” said the older man. “You’re no help to me when you mope around. I know you feel stuck here on Tatooine. Just give me one more year. When our harvest comes in, you can fly off to the Academy.”

“I’m not moping,” said Luke. He was a

young pilot. And he was restless on Tatooine. He did not want to be a farmer, like his uncle. He wanted to be a great pilot, like his father before him. "I just don't see anything worth buying here. It's all a heap of junk."

"Begging your pardon, sir," said Threepio. "But I'm in tiptop condition."

Luke's uncle stopped. "Can you translate languages?"

"That's what I was made for, sir!"

"Can you talk to vaporator machines?"

"Oh, yes, sir! I once worked with load lifters. They speak the same language as vaporators, you know."

"All right. Shut up," said Luke's uncle. He turned away to pay the Jawas. "I'll take that red R2 unit too," he told them.

"Oh, sir," said Threepio, pointing to Artoo. "This R2 unit is in much better condition.

I've worked with him before."

"All right, all right. I'll take him."

So Artoo and Threepio set out for the farm with Luke and his uncle. "Why I stick my neck out for you I'll never know," said Threepio.

Artoo knew—and said so with a beep.

Not far away, Vader's men found the escape pod. They saw, too, the tracks leading away from it. "Droids," said one of them.

His officer nodded. "The princess was pretty smart. But we'll find them. Or else. We can't go back empty-handed. Understand?"

All of them did. Even on this hot planet, they could feel a chill when they thought of Darth Vader's anger.

CHAPTER THREE

The Jawas' gun blast had burned up many of Artoo's wires. All that evening Luke worked to fix him. Now he was finishing up. Suddenly a beam of light flashed out of the little droid's head. At the end of the beam a tiny image of Princess Leia appeared.

"Help me, Obi-Wan Kenobi," the image pleaded. "You are my only hope."

"Who is she?" Luke asked. "And why is she in trouble?"

"I'm really not sure, sir," said Threepio. "She was on our ship when—"

"Help me, Obi-Wan Kenobi," said Leia again. "You are my only hope."

"I know a man named Kenobi. He's a hermit who lives way out among the rocks. But his first name is Ben, not—"

"Help me, Obi-Wan Kenobi…"

"This message is stuck," said Luke. "I want to hear the rest of it." He reached out to touch Artoo's wires. But the little droid let out a loud squeak. Then he gave a few soft beeps.

"He says he's been locked," said Threepio. "To keep him from running away. And the lock is causing a short circuit. That's why he can't get the message out."

"No problem," said Luke, taking the lock off.

Just then his aunt called him to dinner.

"I'll be back in a little while," Luke told the droids. As soon as he went out of one door, Artoo headed for another.

"Stop!" Threepio cried. "Come back! Where are you going?"

"Balloop...beel...glurm...zing...ping!" And Artoo was gone.

Threepio was terribly upset. "I'm sorry, sir!" he said when Luke came back later. "But Artoo ran off! I just couldn't stop him! I'm sure there's something wrong with him. He said he was going to find his master, Obi-Wan Kenobi!"

Luke raced for his landspeeder. "Climb in and let's go!" But then he stopped and thought it over. Darkness had come over the desert. The deadly sand people would be on the prowl. He would have to wait until morning.

CHAPTER FOUR

Just before dawn Luke set out with Threepio. The small flying machine was fast. It sped along above the desert sands, following Artoo's tracks into the rocky country.

"Couldn't you go a little slower, sir?" asked Threepio.

"Relax. I've been flying since I was ten. I could go through these canyons with my eyes shut."

"Oh, don't, sir! Please don't!"

"There he is!"

Artoo was up ahead, moving slowly. He seemed very tired. Luke pulled up. He got out of the landspeeder when Artoo started to beep wildly.

"Sir!" Threepio screamed. "Look out!"

A big Tusken Raider came at Luke from behind a boulder. He was swinging a sharp battle ax. Luke whirled around and blocked it with his rifle. But his gun split in half. He fell backward—and his head hit a rock. Other Raiders rushed in to finish him off. But just then there was a terrible noise. The Raiders drew back. Then they turned and ran in all directions.

Strange! An old man had frightened them off. He bent down beside the fallen boy. Then he touched him. It was a gentle touch. Yet it seemed to have the power to open Luke's eyes. Luke found himself gazing up at the kind face of the hermit, Ben Kenobi.

"Now, then, young Luke Skywalker. What are you doing out here in the wilds?"

"Chasing this droid we just bought. He has a message for someone named Obi-Wan Kenobi...Were you ever called that, Ben?"

"Once...very long ago. But we can't talk about it here. The sand people will be coming back. And there will be many more of them. We must go quickly."

Ben Kenobi's house was built into the rocks. It was small and simple. And there was something very peaceful about it. "Now, then," he said to Artoo. "Why have you been looking for me?"

Artoo's beam began to shine again.

Once more Luke found himself staring at the beautiful princess. "General Kenobi," Leia's image said. "Years ago you served my father on Alderaan. Now he leads the fight to free us from the Empire. Darth Vader has taken my ship. He wants to get back the secret plans for the Emperor's Death Star. I've put them into the memory of this droid. You must get them safely to my father. If you don't, Vader and the Emperor will stamp out the Rebellion. We shall all remain slaves! Help me, Obi-Wan Kenobi. You are my only hope!"

"Who is Darth Vader?" asked Luke.

The old general frowned. "Once he was a Jedi Knight. Like myself...and your father. But he turned to the dark side of the Force."

"My father was a Jedi?"

"Your uncle has hidden it from you, I know. He didn't want you to become a warrior, Luke. Or meet your father's fate."

"What happened to him? How did he die?"

"Vader betrayed us all. He helped the Emperor hunt us down. He used the Force for evil, Luke. Betrayed your father…and murdered him."

"What is this Force?"

"The power that is in all living things, and all around us. It guides the heart of a Jedi. And his hand, too, when he uses his lightsaber. Have you ever seen one?"

"No."

The old man turned and walked over to a chest. He opened it and took out a sword. Suddenly the thing became alive with light. "This was your father's. He wanted me to give it to you when you were old enough to use it. Take this, Luke. Then come with me to Alderaan. Learn about the Force. Let us deliver the plans together and then join the Rebels."

Luke's heart leaped at the old man's words. But how could he go off now with Ben Kenobi? His uncle needed him for the harvest. And he had given his word to stay until then.

"I don't know," Luke said. "I...I have to think. Maybe I should just take you to the nearest spaceport. You can get a ship from there—" He fell silent.

"You must do what you feel is right," said the old man. "Can you take me to the spaceport now?"

"Yes," said Luke.

Moments later he was racing across the desert in his landspeeder with Ben and the droids. Before long he saw smoke rising in the distance. It was the Jawas' sandcrawler—and it was burning! Many dead Jawas lay nearby.

"Tusken Raiders must have done this," said Luke.

Ben studied the tracks. "No. This is the work of Imperial troopers."

"But why?"

Then all at once Luke understood. The soldiers had been searching for Artoo and the plans. "By now they must know who bought the droids from the Jawas!" he cried. "They'll be after my aunt and uncle!"

Luke jumped back into his landspeeder and took off. The landspeeder raced all the way to the farm. But the trip seemed to take hours. At last, up ahead, Luke saw the farm. Or what was left of it. Smoke filled the air. He leaped out of the landspeeder and ran toward the flames. Then he stopped. It was too late, he knew. There was nothing left to keep him here now. The uncle and aunt he loved so dearly were dead.

CHAPTER FIVE

It was a long ride to the spaceport of Mos Eisley. Everywhere, Imperial troopers were on the lookout for the escaped droids. Some of them surrounded the speeder as Luke drove into town.

One trooper shoved his blaster close to Luke's face. "Where did you get these two droids?"

Ben was sitting next to Luke. He gave the man a long look. "These aren't the droids you're looking for," he said in a low voice.

"These aren't the droids we're looking for," the trooper repeated.

"You want us to move along."

"Move along! Move along!" the trooper ordered.

"Amazing!" said Luke as they drove on. "How did you do that?"

"I called upon the Force, Luke. You, too, must learn to find the Force in yourself when you need it. But you must always use your head as well. Be careful as we look for someone to fly us to Alderaan. This is a very dangerous place. Some of the worst riffraff in the galaxy are here."

Some of the weirdest, too. Luke had never seen creatures like the ones who hung around the spacepilots' bar. "Keep your eyes open for more troopers," Ben whispered. "I'll see what I can find out."

Dreaded Imperial stormtroopers!

Princess Leia hides the plans for the Death Star in R2-D2's memory banks.

C-3PO follows R2-D2 to the escape pod.

The Jawas stun R2-D2.

Luke Skywalker shops for a new droid.

Luke zooms over the sand in his landspeeder.

A Tusken Raider attacks Luke.

R2-D2 plays Princess Leia's message
for Ben Kenobi.

Luke returns home—only to find it destroyed!

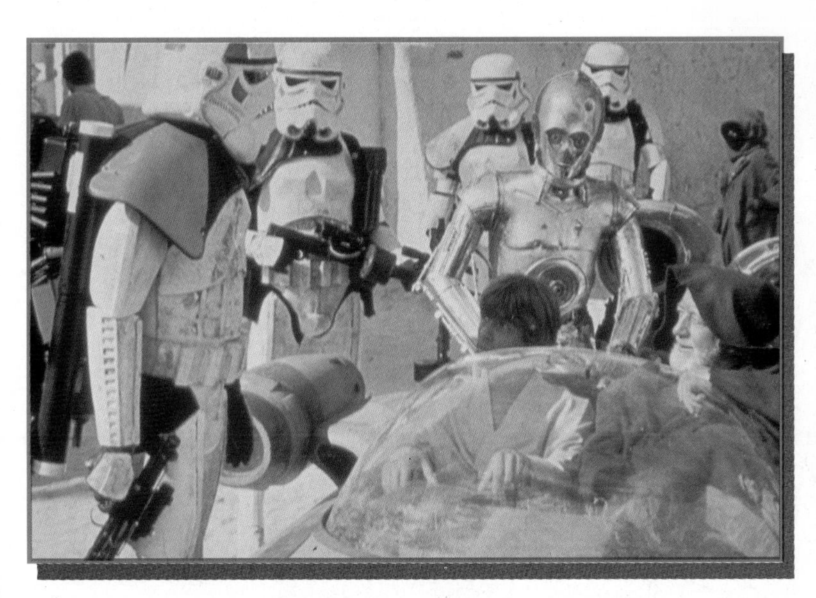

Stormtroopers confront Luke and Ben about the droids.

Han Solo and Chewbacca piloting the *Millennium Falcon*.

Darth Vader holds Princess Leia captive on the Death Star.

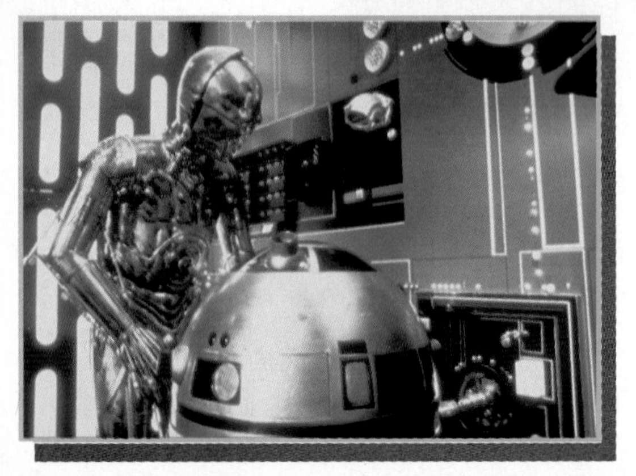

R2-D2 plugs into the Death Star's main computer.

Ben shuts down the tractor beam holding the *Millennium Falcon*.

Vader and Ben duel with lightsabers.

Imperial fighters shoot down attacking Rebel ships.

Princess Leia awards medals to Luke and Han for their bravery.

Ben returned a few minutes later. "I've made a contact," he said quietly. "This is Chewbacca. First mate of a smuggling ship."

The big Wookiee grunted at them. He led them into a darker room and left for a moment. When he came back, a tall, dark-haired man was with him.

"I'm Han Solo," said the man. "Captain of the *Millennium Falcon*. It's the fastest ship going. But getting to Alderaan—with no questions asked—won't be cheap. It'll cost you ten thousand."

Luke jumped to his feet. "Are you kidding? We could almost *buy* a ship for that!"

"But then you don't get *me*." Solo grinned. "And I'm the best."

"Maybe I know someone better!" snapped Luke.

"We're wasting time," said Ben. "Solo, I'll

give you five thousand more than you ask. Two before we leave. The rest when we get there."

Han looked at Chewie. The Wookiee honked. "Okay—we go!" said Han. "Let's have the money."

Ben stood up. "We don't have it with us. We'll be back with it in a little while. Where do we meet you?"

"Docking bay ninety-four. Make it fast. I've got my own problems around here to worry about."

One of the problems showed up just a few minutes later. It was a creature who worked for the gangster Jabba the Hutt. And he was pointing a gun.

Han leaned back. He smiled at the slimy green monster. "Hello, Greedo. Tell Jabba I'm coming up with the money I owe him."

"Too late for that now, Solo. Much too late. You are one dead smuggler."

"Sorry to hear it." And under the table Han pulled the trigger of his blaster.

CHAPTER SIX

Ben and Luke had gone looking for someone to buy the speeder. That took time. They had to keep out of sight whenever troopers went by. At last they found a buyer. Now they had the money to pay Han. But they had something else, too. A shadow. A spy for the Empire was quietly following them.

Han was waiting at the docking bay when they arrived. "Come on. Let's get aboard!"

Just then troopers came rushing in from

everywhere. Han yanked out his blaster and shot back at them. While the troopers ducked for cover, everyone dashed into the *Falcon*.

"Chewie! Get us out of here!"

Chewbacca pulled back on the controls. The *Falcon* blasted off with a roar. But seconds later warships came racing after them.

"We're not getting away!" cried Luke. "I thought you said this old tub was fast!"

"Watch your mouth, kid. It's just got to work itself up to the big jump, that's all."

"That better be soon. They're firing at us!"

"Don't you think I know that?"

Suddenly the *Falcon* began to rock and bounce.

"Do you also know that they're *hitting* us?" said Luke.

Han ignored the question. "Strap yourselves in," he ordered. "Here we go to light-speed!"

In an instant all the stars that had been in front of them seemed to be rushing past. Whole worlds went by. Suns with all their planets. Thousands of them. Then a strange thing happened. The faster the *Falcon* went, the more peaceful everyone inside the ship became.

Yet they were heading straight ahead ...into the very heart of evil.

Torture had not worked on Princess Leia. Darth Vader took her from his ship to the Death Star...and sailed it close to Alderaan.

"Look down there, Princess. Your planet, where millions live. Tell me now where the hidden Rebel base is. Or I shall blow this world to dust."

Thinking fast, the princess tried to argue.

Vader would not listen. "You must decide now!" he growled.

"It's on Dantooine," she lied.

"Good," said the Dark Lord. "But it pleases me to show our power anyway." He turned to his gunners. "Fire!"

"No, no! *Wait!*"

It was too late. A great ray shot out of the mighty space station. It struck the planet below. In an instant, green and lovely Alderaan burst apart…and was no more.

CHAPTER SEVEN

Inside the *Falcon*, Obi-Wan Kenobi shuddered. "Something terrible has happened," he said. "I can feel it in the Force."

"Maybe you're right with that hocus-pocus," called Han from the controls. "We're here—but Alderaan isn't. I think it's been blown away. We better get out of here!"

Then Han saw a great, shining, round ball up ahead. "That's funny," he said. "I don't remember Alderaan having a moon."

"That's a giant space station!" cried Ben. "Turn the ship around. Quickly!"

"I can't!" shouted Han. He worked at the controls. "We're caught in a tractor beam! It's pulling us in!"

"We're trapped!" Luke cried.

"Hey, kid, that's a word I don't like to use."

"What's a better one?"

"Hide!"

Minutes later the *Falcon* was pulled into the Death Star. Then Darth Vader himself came aboard. "This is the same ship that escaped from Tatooine," he told his men. "The droids with the plans must be here somewhere."

The troops searched but found nothing. "The ship is empty, my lord," said an officer. "And I found this captain's log book. It says that everyone left the *Falcon* some time ago."

"That may be," said Vader. But he was

troubled. He felt something in the Force. What was it? "Place guards around this vessel!" he ordered, and left.

As soon as Vader and his men were gone, a secret hatch in the floor opened.

"Now what?" Han wanted to know.

Ben already had a plan. "The beam is like a magnet, holding our ship here. It has to be shut off before the *Falcon* can break free. We have to get into their main computer. It should tell us what to do. But there's no time to lose. We must get the secret plans to the Rebels! I fear for more worlds than Alderaan if we don't."

There were guards to be taken care of first. Ben tricked them into coming inside the ship. Han and Luke took care of them and put on their uniforms. Then, very quietly, everyone slipped out of the *Falcon*.

In the Death Star's huge hangar was a

guardpost. Ben thought he'd find a lead-in there to the main memory bank. The guard inside answered a knock at the door. And walked straight into Chewie's fist.

Threepio found a terminal, and Artoo plugged into a socket. Soon Ben knew exactly where to find a switch to the tractor beam.

"Stay here," he told Luke, who wanted to go with him. "It's best that I do this alone. May the Force be with you!" And he was gone.

Artoo was still at the computer. Now he started to beep with excitement.

"He says he's found the princess!" cried Threepio.

"Where is she?"

"In cellblock twenty-three. On the fifth level. She's to be killed!"

"Han! Chewie! Let's go!" cried Luke.

"Not me, kid. I break *out* of jails—not into them."

"Han, she's rich!"

"Rich?"

"There'll be a big reward!"

"How big?"

"Bigger than you could ever imagine."

"Yeah? Well, I can imagine quite a bit."

"You'll get it!"

"I'd better! You got a plan?"

"We're going to arrest Chewie."

A short while later two troopers and a prisoner stepped off an elevator. A cellblock guard stopped them. "Where are you taking this...thing?"

Chewie didn't much like being called a "thing."

He broke out of the handcuffs and went for the officer. Han took on the other guards. At the same time, Luke raced off to find the princess's cell. Then he blasted his way in.

"I'm Luke Skywalker! I'm here with Ben Kenobi. Come on!" But he and Princess Leia didn't get very far down the hall. Other troopers were coming, firing at Han and Chewie.

"Go back! Back!" Han shouted.

"Back to where?"

"How should I know, kid? It's your show!"

"Some rescue!" snapped the princess. "Follow me!" She grabbed one of Luke's blasters and led them off.

CHAPTER EIGHT

There were tunnels at the bottom of the Death Star. Ben Kenobi moved through them like a ghost. No one saw him. Or if they did, he made them forget. At last he came to a shaft. It went straight up to the top of the space station. Carefully, he made the dangerous climb. Then he reached out and pulled the switch that shut off the tractor beam.

"My work is almost done," he thought as

he climbed down. Returning through the tunnels, he began to sense something. It grew stronger and stronger. "Vader knows that I'm here," Ben told himself. "He's felt my presence in the Force. And now he's waiting for me...at the end of the tunnel."

The old Jedi put his hand on his lightsaber and stopped. From out of the shadows stepped the Dark Lord. His saber flashed on.

"The circle is complete, Obi-Wan. Once I was your student. Now *I* am the master."

"Only the master of evil, Darth."

Obi-Wan lunged for him with his saber. Vader's own sword clashed against it. Obi-Wan thrust again. Vader stopped it again. Now Vader lashed out. Obi-Wan blocked him, but he fell back.

"Your powers are weak, old man."

"You may think so. But if you strike me

down, I shall become strong. Stronger than you ever thought possible."

Back and forth the battle raged. News of it spread among the troopers. They came running from all parts of the Death Star. Soon even the *Falcon* was left unguarded.

Ben's friends fought their way back through the Death Star. They looked for Ben. And then they saw the duel going on in the tunnel. Han tapped Luke on the shoulder. "Come on, kid. We can't help him. He's doing this for us. Let's go!"

But Luke couldn't bring himself to move.

Leia pleaded with him too. "You're letting him down if you stay. It's the plans that count now! We've got to save the Rebellion!"

Just then Obi-Wan Kenobi turned his head. He seemed to be looking straight at Luke. A smile was on his face. This was Vader's chance. With the speed of light he slashed at Ben. The blow should have cut the old man in half. It sliced right through his robe. But the Jedi was gone. There was nothing left of him. Just two pieces of cloth lying on the floor.

Luke thought he heard a voice whispering in his ear. Ben's voice. "Run, Luke," it said. "Run!"

Troopers were firing at them now. Luke leaped into the ship after the two droids. Han slammed the hatch. "Okay, Chewie! Hit it!" he shouted. The power blazed on. There was no tractor beam to hold the *Falcon* back now! It blasted free into open space.

Luke had grown to love Ben Kenobi. And now Ben was gone forever. The young man was lost in unhappiness. He did not even see Vader's fighters coming after them.

"Get to the guns!" Han shouted.

The Imperials closed in from all directions. Their lasers blasted. Chewie flew the *Falcon* while the others fought. Han fired. Luke fired. Two enemy ships went spinning out of control.

"We've beat 'em!" Han laughed. "The rest are turning back."

The princess shook her head. "They're letting us get away. This was too easy."

"Easy!"

"Vader wants to follow us to the Rebel base and blow it apart."

"Then why go there?"

"So you can get that big reward Luke promised you! What else?" snapped Leia. Then she gave him the directions to the Rebel base. Han punched the controls and the *Falcon* went into lightspeed. When they came out of it, a tiny moon lay below them.

CHAPTER NINE

Leia ran to her generals as soon as the *Falcon* landed. "Hurry!" she told them. "Vader's tracking us here in the Death Star. We don't have much time—it'll blow us apart as soon as it gets here." She pointed to Artoo. "This droid has the plans showing how the Death Star was built. We've got to use them. We've got to figure out a way to attack the Death Star before it's too late!"

The scientists rushed off with Artoo.

They studied the plans of the Death Star. "There's no way we can destroy this monster," said one of them. "We're done for."

"No, wait!" cried another. "Look there!" He pointed to a tiny opening on the surface of the huge space station. "See that vent? If one torpedo could get in there—BLAM! It would go straight to the main reactor!"

"But that's an impossible shot. And look what a ship would have to do to get near it. Fly through that metal canyon! It's too narrow. There'd be no room to move left or right. The ship would be a sitting duck for the enemy!"

"It's the only chance we've got."

Leia's officers agreed. They called their pilots together. "You'll go after the Death Star in two groups. Red Wing protects Gold Wing. Gold Wing goes after the target."

A Rebel captain rushed in with news.

"Death Star coming toward us. Time of arrival, fifteen minutes!"

"Everyone to your ships! And may the Force be with you!"

Luke ran over to Han. "We need you. Are you coming with us?"

"Not me, kid. You guys are going to kill yourselves. I got my reward. I want to stay alive to spend it."

So it was good-bye, then. Sadly Luke climbed into his little fighter. Han watched him blast off with the other Rebel pilots in Red Wing. Then he heard Chewie growling behind him. "What are you barking at, you big ape? I know what I'm doing!"

The two waves of Rebel ships streaked toward the Death Star. Lasers started to blaze away at them from the surface. Gold Wing's ships were being hit. They were turning into balls of flame. "Let's knock out those guns!" called the leader of Red Wing over his mike.

Luke swooped down with the others—and blasted away at the Death Star's cannons. Just as he was pulling up again, he saw the Imperial ships. They were closing in on the Gold Wing fighters.

Inside the first ship was Darth Vader himself. Nothing could escape him. Again and again he took aim. One after another, the Rebel ships exploded.

Now only Gold Leader was left. He headed for the canyon. He was making a run for the vent! But Vader was after him, blazing away. Gold Leader's ship blew apart.

Luke had had enough. "I'm going in!" he cried over the mike.

Straight down he dived for the canyon.

Two other Rebel ships fell in behind him to give him cover. Luke came out of his dive between the walls. Now he had to go straight ahead. There was no room for any mistake. The slightest move this way or that would smash his craft to pieces. He locked the target in on the computer. Then he threw on all the speed he could get. Suddenly he heard explosions behind him.

"I'm hit!" called out one of the Rebel pilots covering him. "Got to pull out!"

"They're coming in on me fast!" shouted the other. "Luke! I can't hold them for you!"

There was a scream. Then silence.

An Imperial ship was behind Luke now. And it was faster than his own. "Artoo!" Luke yelled to the little droid, who had come with him. "Try and increase the power!"

But it was too late. Vader's lasers lashed

out. Luke's ship took a hit that nearly sent it into the wall. The craft was shaking now. It was hard to keep it steady. Even if he made it as far as the target, how could the computer help him hit it?

Vader wasn't going to give him the chance to find out. One more blast of his lasers would finish Luke off. "I have you now," he hissed.

But he never got to press the trigger. From out of nowhere came a burst of laser fire. It slammed into Vader's craft. One of his wings was damaged. Now Vader could do nothing but try to keep from crashing. His ship spun out of the narrow canyon, turning over and over.

"Yahoo!" Han yelled into his mike. "You're all clear, kid. Blow it away!"

Luke's ship was rattling. How could he hope to find that tiny opening? And then send a torpedo right through it into the Death Star?

But he had to! Already the Death Star was over the Rebel base. In only a few short seconds it would let loose all of its fury. . .

This time Luke *knew* he was hearing Ben's voice.

"Shut off the computer, Luke. And remember the Force. Trust the *Force,* Luke."

Luke smiled to himself as he reached to turn off the computer. The Force would guide him. He knew it now.

Inside the space station a countdown was going on. Five seconds to go until the Death Star blew up the Rebel base. "*Four... three...two...*"

And then there *was* an explosion.

Luke got away just in time. He looked back over his shoulder. In a blinding flash of light, the Death Star burst into a billion pieces.

"Okay, everybody," Luke called into his mike. "Let's go home!"

CHAPTER TEN

Threepio was very upset. He saw Artoo being carried out of Luke's ship. The little droid had been badly hurt.

The young Jedi put his arm over Threepio's shoulder. "They'll fix him up again. He'll be all right."

And so he was. Artoo was as good as new when Han and Luke got their medals from Princess Leia. Threepio sighed. Chewbacca grunted. And Artoo rocked and beeped with happiness.

This was a time of victory and of warm friendship. But soon another time would come.

A time when the Empire would strike back...

Larry Weinberg has been both a lawyer and a playwright, but now spends almost all of his time writing for children. He is also a devoted Star Wars fan and has seen each of the Star Wars movies so many times that he's lost count. Among his many books are *Star Wars: The Making of the Movie; Guess a Rhyme; Frankenstein;* and *Dragonslayer: The Storybook Based on the Movie.*

Mr. Weinberg lives in Woodstock, New York.

Continue the fight against the Empire in the next book from the Classic Star Wars® trilogy:

THE EMPIRE STRIKES BACK™

"Attention! Attention! Imperial Star Destroyers coming out of hyperspace in Sector Four!"

"Close the energy shield!" Princess Leia ordered. "And give it all the power we've got!"

Luke climbed into his armored snowspeeder and prepared for lift-off.

Then the loudspeaker blared again.

"This is Forward Post Three. The Imperials are landing." The voice grew shaky. "Only they're not soldiers. They're like huge animals! Our lasers are bouncing right off them!"

Luke frowned. They had to slow down the Imperial attack long enough for the transports to get away. Otherwise, the Rebellion was doomed!

If you enjoyed the out-of-this-world adventures in Star Wars, then you'll love the whip-cracking exploits of Young Indiana Jones™!

YOUNG INDIANA JONES BOOKS
(original novels)

Young Indiana Jones and the...

1. Plantation Treasure
2. Tomb of Terror
3. Circle of Death
4. Secret City
5. Princess of Peril
6. Gypsy Revenge
7. Ghostly Riders
8. Curse of the Ruby Cross
9. Titanic Adventure
10. Lost Gold of Durango
11. Face of the Dragon
12. Journey to the Underworld
13. Mountain of Fire
14. Pirates' Loot
15. Eye of the Tiger

And coming soon:

16. Mask of the Madman